John Dougherty

Stinkbomb & Ketchup-Face

and the Badness of Badgers

Illustrated by David Tazzyman (Illustrator of Mr Gum).

World's Best Badger

OXFORD
UNIVERSITY PRESS

OXFORD
UNIVERSITY PRESS

Great Clarendon Street, Oxford OX2 6DP

Oxford University Press is a department of the University of Oxford.
It furthers the University's objective of excellence in research, scholarship,
and education by publishing worldwide in

Oxford   New York

Auckland   Cape Town   Dar es Salaam   Hong Kong   Karachi
Kuala Lumpur   Madrid   Melbourne   Mexico City   Nairobi
New Delhi   Shanghai   Taipei   Toronto

With offices in

Argentina   Austria   Brazil   Chile   Czech Republic   France   Greece
Guatemala   Hungary   Italy   Japan   Poland   Portugal   Singapore
South Korea   Switzerland   Thailand   Turkey   Ukraine   Vietnam

Oxford is a registered trade mark of Oxford University Press
in the UK and in certain other countries

Database right Oxford University Press (maker)

First published 2014

British Library Cataloguing in Publication Data

Data available

ISBN: 978-0-19-273449-5

5 7 9 10 8 6

Printed in Great Britain
Paper used in the production of this book is a natural,
recyclable product made from wood grown in sustainable forests
The manufacturing process conforms to the environmental
regulations of the country of origin.

For my favourite antipodean piglets, Genevieve & Holly,
with love from your Uncle John.

And—as always—for the original Stinkbomb &
Ketchup-Face, Noah & Cara, with all my love.
More than ever, this one's for you. J.D.

For Oscar and Alice. D.T.

Enchanted
Wood

Stream

Royal Palace

chapter 1

In which our heroes wake up, and a startling discovery is made

It was early morning, and dawn was breaking over the peaceful little island of Great Kerfuffle. The golden sun peeped over the horizon, checked to make sure no one was looking, and slowly climbed into the blue sky.

And far below, in a tall tree in the garden of a lovely house high on a hillside above the tiny village of Loose Chippings, a blackbird cleared its throat and broke forth into song to greet the new day.

Inside the lovely house, in a beautiful pink bedroom, a little girl opened her eyes and leapt out of bed. Dashing to the window, she flung the shutters wide open. The sunlight streamed in, bringing with it the sweet smell of blossoms on the morning breeze, and, as if in greeting, the tree waved gently and rustled its leaves. There, on the nearest branch, so close she could almost touch it, perched the blackbird, trilling merrily.

'Oi! Blackbird! Shut your beak!'

yelled the little girl, and she threw a shoe at it.

The shoe bounced off the branch and fell to the ground, where it was picked up by a passing cat. The blackbird stuck out its tongue and blew a **defiant raspberry**; then it flew away. The

 little girl stomped grumpily back to her bed and shut her eyes. But it was no good: she couldn't get back to sleep. After a few minutes, she tried actually getting into the bed and lying down; but that didn't help either. So then she decided to go and jump on her brother's face.

Seconds later, in the bedroom just across the landing, the little girl's brother pulled one of her toes out of his left nostril and groaned wearily.

'Morning, Stinkbomb!' said the little girl cheerily, sitting down with a **flump!** on his tummy. 'Time to get up!'

'Why?' said Stinkbomb grouchily.

'Because,' said the little girl, 'it's a beautiful morning, and the sun is shining, and we can play games and have adventures, and if you don't get up I'm going to put porridge down your trousers forever, so there.'

Stinkbomb thought about this. The idea of having porridge put down his trousers forever certainly sounded interesting, but on balance he wasn't sure if he fancied it. So he decided to get up.

As he did, he made a disturbing discovery. On his bedroom floor lay a small ceramic pig with its feet in the air and a hole in its tummy.

'Oi! Ketchup-Face!' he said crossly. 'Have you been raiding my piggy bank?'

Ketchup-Face shook her head. 'Nope,' she said.

'Well, *somebody* has!' said Stinkbomb. 'Look!' He picked up the empty pig and shook it. A solitary penny fell out and landed with a little *thunk* on the carpet. 'I had a **whole tenner** in there, and it's gone!'

Ketchup-Face shrugged. 'Wasn't me.'

Stinkbomb scratched his head. His sister had

many faults, but telling lies wasn't one of them. 'Well, then,' he said, 'it must have been the badgers.'

Ketchup-Face thought about this. She wasn't really sure what badgers were, so she just nodded and tried to look wise. Then she changed her mind and asked, 'What's a badger?'

'It's a, it's a, well, *you* know,' said Stinkbomb. 'They dig holes in the lawn, and eat all the worms, and they knock over dustbins, and frighten chickens, and drive too fast.'

'Oh,' said Ketchup-Face. 'And do they empty piggy banks as well?'

'Probably,' Stinkbomb said knowledgeably. 'It sounds like the sort of thing they *would* do.'

Ketchup-Face scratched her head. It was quite a pretty head, except when the front bit was covered with **ketchup** and **chocolate** and **jam** and **mud**. Just at the moment it was clean, but it was a fair bet that by the end of Chapter Four it would be filthy again.

'Does it?' she asked.

Stinkbomb tutted in a big-brotherly kind of way. 'Of course it does,' he said. 'Think about it. They do **bad** things, 'cos they're **bad**gers. If they weren't **bad**, they'd just be **gers**. I bet our bin's been knocked over as well.'

Ketchup-Face opened the window and looked outside. Sure enough, the family dustbin was lying on its side in the garden, giving every indication of having been badgered.

'Gosh,' Ketchup-Face said, impressed, 'I suppose that proves it. The badgers have taken your tenner. What are we going to do about it?'

Stinkbomb drew himself upright. Then he drew himself sitting down, and then he drew himself winning a race and getting a medal, and then he drew a dinosaur having a bath; and then he put his pencil down and said, 'I'll tell you what we're going to do. We're going to see the king.'

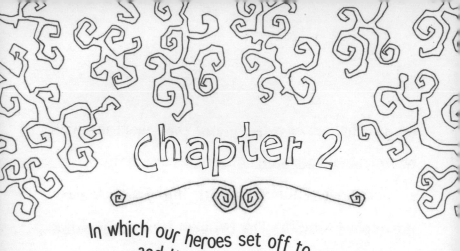

chapter 2

In most stories, if the heroes were to set off to see the king, you'd expect their journey to take a really long time. **Chapters** and **chapters** and **chapters**, probably, in which they'd have adventures, and fight dragons and giant spiders. They'd get lost in the forest, and nearly get eaten by witches, and have to solve mysterious riddles before they could cross rivers or ravines, and all that kind of stuff. And it'd probably rain as well, and they wouldn't have brought their coats or sandwiches or anything.

Fortunately for Stinkbomb and Ketchup-Face, the nearest king lived only half a mile away. It was just five minutes on the number 47 bus if you had 50p each; but Stinkbomb and Ketchup-Face didn't have any money, so they set off through the fields.

It was a truly beautiful day. The sun beamed down on them like a kindly uncle, the trees waved like friendly flags, and all around them the birds twittered and tweeted like a tiny feathered choir. All of nature was at play: they saw newts playing **leap** frog and frogs playing **leap** newt; bunnies playing **leap** squirrel and squirrels playing **leap** bunny; foxes playing

leap pig and pigs playing **squash**fox, because pigs aren't very good at leaping, and they're quite **big**. They saw a snake basking in the sunshine, lambs frolicking in the pasture, and a shy deer in a false moustache peeping through the hedgerow. It was all so lovely that it made Ketchup-Face want to sing, and—since making up songs was one of her favourite things to do—that's exactly what she did.

This is what she sang:

'Blueberry jam

Blueberry jam

Blueberry jam, blueberry jam

Blueberry, blueberry, blueberry jam

Bluey, bluey, bluey, bluey

Bluey, bluey, blueberry jam
Blueberry jam

Blueberry *jam*

Blueberry

jaaaaaa

aaaaaa

aaam!!!!!°°°°°

'That's a song about blueberry jam,' she added.

'Very nice,' said Stinkbomb. 'What's it called?'

Ketchup-Face thought about this. 'Ummm . . . Blueberry Jam,' she said. "Cos it's about blueberry jam.'

Stinkbomb nodded wisely. 'I see,' he said. He paused, tactfully, for he liked to encourage his little sister when she wasn't jumping on his face and sticking her toes up his nose, but he felt there was something about the song that left room for improvement. 'Do you think it might be a bit . . . samey?' he said eventually.

Ketchup-Face **scratched** her head. 'I see what you mean,' she said. 'Maybe I should put some other kinds of jam in it as well.'

So on they went, with Ketchup-Face trying out different kinds of jam in her song, and Stinkbomb sticking his fingers in his ears, until at last they caught sight of the palace.

Ketchup-Face stopped singing and pointed. 'There it is,' she said happily.

'What did you say?' said Stinkbomb.

'There it is,' repeated Ketchup-Face.

'What did you say???' said Stinkbomb.

`'I said, there it is!'`

yelled Ketchup-Face.

'What did you say???'

shouted Stinkbomb.

Ketchup-Face tugged at Stinkbomb's elbows until his fingers popped out of his ears again. 'I said, there it is,' she explained.

'Oh,' said Stinkbomb. 'Why didn't you say so? And by the way,' he added, 'why are you **hopping?**'

Ketchup-Face looked down at her feet. 'Because I threw one of my shoes at a blackbird,' she said happily. 'Come on!'

And off she **hippity-hopped** again, with Stinkbomb **pootling** along behind her, until they reached the palace.

Hippity-Hop

chapter 3

In which we learn a little history

Not many children live only half a mile from a real king; but then not many children live near the tiny village of **Loose Chippings** on the little island of **Great Kerfuffle**. **Loose Chippings** is the capital village of **Great Kerfuffle**, which is too small to have a capital city or even a capital town; but even so, **Great Kerfuffle** is very rare among little islands, because it has its very own king all to itself.

The reason for this dates back to the **Wars of the Roses**. There was an argument between **King Richard III** and **King Henry VII** as to which of them was really the king, and they agreed that the best way to find out who was right was to put lots of men in a field and get them to hit each other with pointy things.

What most people don't know is that there was a third man who thought he was king. He was known as **King Isabel the Confused**, and he kept turning up at battles and trying to join in. The problem was that **King Isabel** hadn't really got the hang of battling, and he and his soldiers just ended up getting in the way and shouting things like, 'Put that pointy thing down! You'll have someone's eye out if you're not careful!'

King Richard

The effect was rather like when a small dog tries to take part in a football match. The dog has no chance of winning, but it makes it very

Put that pointy thing down!
You'll have someone's eye out
if you're not careful!

King Henry

King Isabel
the
Confused

difficult for anyone else to, either. So, in the end, **King Richard** and **King Henry** decided that the only way to get on with the battle was to give **King Isabel** a little kingdom of his very own, as long as he promised to go away and stop being a pain.

The kingdom they gave him was, of course, **Great Kerfuffle**, which at that time was at the very tip of the Cornish peninsula; and as soon as **King Isabel** had been crowned as its king, **King Henry** tiptoed down in the dead of night, sawed it off, and sent it floating out to sea. **King Richard** would have helped, but he couldn't on account of having lost the battle, and so being extremely dead.

And that is why **Great Kerfuffle** has its very own king.

The king who was now on the throne was a great great great great great great great great great great great on and on forever lots and lots of times great great great this is getting a bit boring great great great great great great grandson of **King Isabel the Confused**, and his name was **King Sandra**; or, at least, it had been until recently. However, he had worried that perhaps **King Sandra** was a silly name, and had decided to change it to something more sensible.

Unfortunately, he had made the mistake of asking the citizens of **Great Kerfuffle** to choose his new, sensible name, which is why he was now known as **King Toothbrush Weasel**.

King Toothbrush Weasel lived, of course, in a palace—the very palace that Stinkbomb and Ketchup-Face had just reached.

You remember. At the end of Chapter Two.

And now it's the end of Chapter Three.

King Toothbrush Weasel's palace wasn't very big. In fact, it was about the size of a small cottage. It had pretty little towers with thatched turrets, and dinky little battlements, and the sweetest little sentry box you've ever seen; and in the little sentry box the entire army of Great Kerfuffle was standing guard.

You might think that it would be a bit of a **squeeze**, fitting an entire army into one little sentry box; but you'd be wrong. Great Kerfuffle was, of course, a very small kingdom, and it couldn't afford a big army with lots of soldiers. In fact, there was only one soldier in the army of Great Kerfuffle, and he was a small cat called Malcolm the Cat.

Stinkbomb and Ketchup-Face looked down at him. He was a small grey cat with one shoe and a little red soldier's jacket. He also had one of those big, tall, furry bearskin hats, just like the guards outside Buckingham Palace have, but he never wore it because it would have covered him completely and left him unable to move. Instead, he was lying on it to make himself look **taller** without actually having to stand up.

'And what do *you* want?' said Malcolm the Cat, in a tone of voice that suggested he wasn't really interested unless it involved a can-opener and a tin of cat food.

'We'd like to see King Toothbrush Weasel, please,' said Ketchup-Face.

'Why?' asked Malcolm the Cat.

'Because the badgers have stolen my tenner,' Stinkbomb said.

Malcolm the Cat sat up and stared at them both without blinking, until they felt a bit uncomfortable. 'All right, then,' he said eventually. 'You can knock on the door.' Then, as Stinkbomb raised his hand to knock, he said, 'Actually, you can't.'

Stinkbomb dropped his hand. 'Why not?' he said.

Malcolm the Cat looked at him, as if thinking. 'No, I suppose you can,' he said.

Stinkbomb's hand went to the knocker.

said Malcolm the Cat.

Stinkbomb stopped and looked at him.

'Oh, go on then,' said Malcolm the Cat. As Stinkbomb raised his hand again, he added, 'Sorry, you can't after all. My mistake.'

'But . . . ' began Stinkbomb.

'Oh, all right,' Malcolm the Cat said. After

a pause, during which Stinkbomb looked at him suspiciously, he said, 'No, go on. Really. You can knock on the door. You have my official permission.'

'Really?' said Stinkbomb.

'Really,' said Malcolm the Cat. 'Honest. Go on.'

Stinkbomb raised his hand to the knocker.

'Oh, wait,' said Malcolm the Cat. 'Sorry. You can't knock on the door after all.'

Ketchup-Face gave Malcolm the Cat the special glare she reserved for especially annoying people, and parents who wouldn't give her chocolate. 'What are you doing?' she asked.

'Sorry,' said Malcolm the Cat. 'Just playing with you. Force of habit. I won't do it again. You can knock on the door now. Oh, whoops,' he added, as Stinkbomb went once more to knock, 'my mistake. You can't.'

It could have gone on like this for some time if Stinkbomb hadn't remembered that he had a fish in his pocket. Stinkbomb was the sort of boy whose pockets were always full of things that might come in handy later; and it occurred to him that if you are dealing with an uncooperative cat, the best way to win it round is with a nice fat fish.

So he pulled the fish out of his pocket, and with a mighty WHAM! he knocked Malcolm the Cat off the bearskin hat with it. Before Malcolm the Cat could pick himself up again, Stinkbomb had knocked on the palace door.

Chapter 5

In which our heroes meet the King

Immediately they heard the sound of footsteps from inside the palace, quiet at first, but **getting louder**. They waited, both of them feeling the warm sun on their backs and the soft breeze in their hair, and Stinkbomb feeling a gentle tugging at his side, which turned out to be Malcolm the Cat trying to climb into his pocket to get the fish.

Eventually, the door opened, and there stood King Toothbrush Weasel, wearing a yellow checked dressing gown on which was pinned a little badge that said (Butler).

'Yes?' said King Toothbrush Weasel.

'Hello, King Toothbrush Weasel,' said Ketchup-Face, grinning her special grin that she kept for important people. She was particularly proud of this grin at the moment, as it showed the gap where she had recently lost a tooth.

King Toothbrush Weasel gave Ketchup-Face a stern look. 'I am not King Toothbrush Weasel,' he said firmly, tapping the little badge that said (Butler). 'I am the butler. Now, what do you want?'

'We've come to see King Toothbrush Weasel,' said Stinkbomb.

'And who shall I say is calling?' asked King Toothbrush Weasel.

'Ketchup-Face and Stinkbomb,' said Ketchup-Face, who was tired of always being second.

'Stinkbomb and Ketchup-Face,' corrected Stinkbomb, who liked to insist on his rights as the older child.

'Ketchup-Face and Stinkbomb and Stinkbomb and Ketchup-Face,' repeated King Toothbush Weasel. 'Come in. Oh,' he added, 'and do get out of the boy's pocket, Malcolm the Cat. You're supposed to be on guard duty.'

They entered the palace, and found them-selves in a small and cluttered entrance hall. King Toothbrush Weasel **squeezed** past a bicycle which was leaning against the radiator, said, 'Please follow me,' and began walking on the spot, at first thumping his feet on the floor as **loudly** as he could, but getting gradually quieter.

Stinkbomb and Ketchup-Face looked at each other, puzzled. King Toothbrush Weasel glanced over his shoulder at them and halted.

'Do come along,' he said.

'But you're not going anywhere,' Ketchup-Face pointed out. 'You're just walking on the spot and making your footsteps quieter.'

King Toothbrush Weasel turned indignantly. 'I am not walking on the spot,' he said. 'I am walking down a very long corridor in a large and impressive palace! And my footsteps are getting quieter because I am getting further away. Now, come along!'

Stinkbomb and Ketchup-Face shrugged and began to walk on the spot. Satisfied, King Toothbrush Weasel turned again, and led the way without actually going anywhere.

Before very long, they reached a door that they'd been standing beside the whole time.

'Please wait here,' King Toothbrush Weasel said, 'and I shall ask if His Majesty will see you.'

He stepped through the door, and Stinkbomb and Ketchup-Face heard him say: 'Ketchup-Face and Stinkbomb and Stinkbomb and Ketchup-Face to see you, your Majesty.'

And then they heard him say, 'Oh, dear. It's so very, very busy being a king, you know. I was just about to do some busy kingly things, and look at some royal bits of paper, and stuff like that; but I suppose the needs of my subjects must come first. Do show them in.'

And then they heard him say, 'Very good, your Majesty.'

He popped his head out and said, 'King Tooth-brush Weasel will see you now.'

Stinkbomb and Ketchup-Face went in, and waited politely while King Toothbrush Weasel took off the badge that said (Butler), put on a small crown and a badge that said (King), and sat down on a comfy armchair that was trimmed with tinsel and had a label on it saying [Throne].

'Welcome, loyal subjects,' he said. Then he added worriedly, 'You are loyal subjects, I suppose? I wouldn't like to think you were the disloyal sort. Are you loyal subjects?'

'Oh, yes,' said Stinkbomb.

'What's "loyal subjects"?' asked Ketchup-Face. 'Ow,' she added, as Stinkbomb elbowed her in the ribs. 'What'd you do that for? I only asked, 'cos

he said, and anyway, OW,' she went on, as Stink-bomb elbowed her again. 'Oh, all right, yes we are, whatever it is, as long as it doesn't involve spinach.'

King Toothbrush Weasel looked relieved. 'Oh, good,' he said. 'Now,' he continued, smiling at Ketchup-Face, 'you must be Ketchup-Face and Stinkbomb; and you,' he went on, turning to Stinkbomb, 'must be Stinkbomb and Ketchup-Face. You're very young to be coming to the palace all by yourselves. Haven't you brought your parents with you?'

'No, your Majesty,' said Stinkbomb.

'They like to keep out of the way when we're in a story,' explained Ketchup-Face. ''Cos parents spoil stories if they're in them. They just hang around stopping you having adventures and making sure you wash your hands before you touch anything.'

'Very wise,' said King Toothbrush Weasel. Then he sat up straight and looked at her. 'Wait a minute,' he said. 'Do you mean you're in a story now? This minute?'

'Oh, yes,' said Ketchup-Face. 'You can tell 'cos of all the chapters and page numbers and stuff.'

'But . . . but . . . am *I* in the story too?' asked King Toothbrush Weasel worriedly.

'Yup!' said Ketchup-Face happily.

'Yes, your Majesty,' Stinkbomb agreed. 'You don't mind, do you?'

'But I'm in my dressing gown!' said King Toothbrush Weasel. 'I can't be in a story in my dressing gown! Just wait here a minute!'

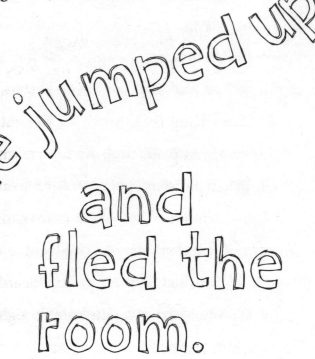

And he jumped up and fled the room.

chapter 6

In which King Toothbrush Weasel goes upstairs to get dressed, and comes back down again

Upstairs, King Toothbrush Weasel put on a nice pair of red pants with golden crowns all over them. Then he chose some purple trousers, and a white shirt, and a red velvet robe trimmed with pretend fur, and got dressed. He went to the dressing table, brushed his long golden beard, and put it on. Finally he combed his hair, straightened his crown, and went downstairs again.

'Right,' he said, as he entered, 'What did you two want to see me about?'

'Well, your Majesty,' Stinkbomb said, 'we wanted to ask for your help, because the badgers have stolen a tenner out of my piggy bank.'

'Badgers?'

said King Toothbrush Weasel. 'Impossible! There are no badgers in the kingdom of Great Kerfuffle! I banned them all by royal decree!'

'Do you think the badgers know that?' asked Ketchup-Face.

'Of course they do,' said King Toothbrush Weasel. 'Anyway, I'd have noticed if Great Kerfuffle was full of badgers, all **galumphing** about being too heavy, and spiking things with those big horns on the ends of their noses.'

'Um, actually I think that sounds more like rhinoceroses,' said Stinkbomb.

'No, no, no,' said King Toothbrush Weasel. 'Rhinoceroses are those little creatures that go "squeak" and eat cheese, and are frightened of the army!'

'I thought those were mouses,' said Ketchup-Face.

'Nonsense!' said King Toothbrush Weasel. 'I'll prove it to you!' He went to the bookshelf, took down a book called *How to Identify a Rhinoceros*, and leafed through it.

'Oh,' he said after a minute. 'It does appear that I might have banned rhinoceroses instead of badgers. Oh, well, never mind. I'll just have to send someone on a mission to drive all badgers from the kingdom. You'll do. Off you go.'

chapter 7

In which our heroes set off on their quest

A minute later, Stinkbomb and Ketchup-Face found themselves leaving the palace with no clear idea of where to go or how to get there, and a firm instruction from King Toothbrush Weasel to rid the kingdom of every badger within its borders by lunchtime.

Stinkbomb was a bit annoyed by this turn of events, but Ketchup-Face was untroubled.

'Don't worry, Stinkbomb,' she said cheerfully. 'We've been sent on a quest by the king, so probably something will happen to help us.'

'Like what?' Stinkbomb grumped. It was nearly mid-morning, and he'd only had one breakfast and no snacks, so he was a bit out of sorts.

'Oh, you know,' said Ketchup-Face. 'We'll probably meet some animals that're in trouble and need help, and we'll help them 'cos we're kind and nice, and then they'll give us a magical thing that'll help us when we need help, and then everyone'll have been helped and it'll all be nice.'

Stinkbomb rolled his êyês. 'Don't be silly,' he said. 'That sort of thing only happens in stories.'

'But we *are* in a story,' Ketchup-Face pointed out.

'Oh, yeah,' said Stinkbomb. 'I forgot.'

And, just at that moment, they heard a rather bored voice saying, 'Help. Oh, help. Oh, deary me, help.'

'Told you,' said Ketchup-Face.

They followed the sound of the voice until it led them to a small grey cat in a red soldier's jacket.

'Oh, help,' said the cat, without much enthusiasm. 'Help, help, help, oh help, help. Help.'

'Hello, poor, dear, sweet little cat,' said Ketchup-Face. 'Whatever can be the matter?'

'Oh, help,' said the cat flatly. 'Help, help, help; for my tail is tangled up with this bit of grass and I cannot get free.'

'Really?' said Stinkbomb. 'Your tail is tangled up with a bit of grass?'

The cat just shrugged.

Quickly, Ketchup-Face got down on one knee and freed the cat—a task which, it has to be said, required no effort at all.

'There!' she said. 'And now you are free, little cat!'

'Oh, hooray,' said the cat, with no more emotion than before, and twitching its tail only a little. 'I am free. Hurrah, hurrah, hurrah. Hurrah. Oh, how can I ever thank you.'

'Well,' said Ketchup-Face, 'since you ask, you could give us a magical item to help us on our quest.'

The cat stared at her without blinking, in what can only be described as a sarcastic manner. 'Oh, what a good idea,' it said. 'Why didn't I think of that.' And then it stared some more.

'So . . . ' said Stinkbomb, after a long and awkward pause. 'Is that what you're going to do?'

'I suppose so,' said the cat reluctantly. 'Here. Because you have saved me from this terrible and dangerous bit of grass, I shall give you . . . this shoe.'

It produced a rather familiar-looking item of footwear and offered it to Ketchup-Face.

'Why, thank you, little cat,' said Ketchup-Face, reaching out to take it.

Just as she was about to take it, the cat snatched it away. 'Oh, sorry,' it said. 'Maybe that wasn't the thing I was supposed to give you after all. Let me think. Oh, yes, it was. Here you are.'

It held out the shoe once again. Ketchup-Face reached for it. The cat snatched it away.

As it held out the shoe a third time, it noticed Stinkbomb's hand moving towards his pocket. Hurriedly it dropped the shoe on the grass.

'Thank you, sweet little cat,' said Ketchup-Face, picking it up. 'And how will this magic shoe help me?'

'Well,' said the cat, 'if ever you are in danger . . .'

'Yes?' said Ketchup-Face.

' . . . you can put it on and run away. It's quicker than hopping,' said the cat, and it turned and disappeared into the long grass with no apparent fear at all of getting its tail entangled again.

'Told you!' said Ketchup-Face happily, tying the shoe round her neck so it wouldn't get lost, and then **hopping** on ahead once more, singing to herself. Stinkbomb followed on behind, stopping occasionally to pick up an interesting thing and put it in his pocket.

After a while, Stinkbomb said, 'We don't know if we're going the right way, you know.'

'Don't worry,' said Ketchup-Face. 'I expect the next animal we meet will be able to tell us.'

And, just at that moment, they heard another little voice saying,

but this one sounded as if it really meant it.

chapter 8

In which our heroes offer help and are helped in return

'Help!' shouted the little voice again; and as they got closer they could hear frantic splashing noises as well.

'This way!' said Stinkbomb, and ran ahead, with Ketchup-Face hopping along behind him. Soon they came to a grassy bank which sloped down to a stream; and there they saw a heartbreaking sight. Struggling for dear life, upside-down in the water and clearly unable to swim, was a little shopping trolley waving its wheels helplessly in the air.

`Don't worry, little shopping trolley! We'll save you!'

shouted Ketchup-Face, as she and Stinkbomb plunged down the bank and into the raging torrent, which came all the way up to their ankles.

Together, they pulled the trolley out and set it upright, placing it carefully on its wheels on the bank.

'Oh, thank you! Thank you!' gasped the shopping trolley. 'You have saved me! How can I ever repay you?'

'Well,' said Ketchup-Face, 'we're on a quest to find the badgers. I don't suppose you know where they live, do you?'

'Why, yes, I do!' said the little shopping trolley happily. 'They live in the next valley, by a magical stream in the middle of an enchanted wood, just next to a small block of flats. Jump into my basket and I will take you there.'

Stinkbomb and Ketchup-Face scrambled into the basket, and at once the little shopping trolley began to race up the grassy bank.

It was terribly exciting. Imagine going on a magical horse ride, on the most beautiful horse you have ever seen.

Now imagine that the horse has got a **squeaky wheel**, and a saddle made out of hard wire that makes a criss-cross pattern on your bottom.

Now imagine that the horse can't go in a straight line, and keeps veering off to one side.

And now imagine that the horse isn't a horse at all, but is in fact a little shopping trolley.

That's what it was like.

Stinkbomb and Ketchup-Face thought it was great. Stinkbomb invented a game called **Bugcatcher**, which involved holding his mouth open and seeing how many bugs he could catch. He gave himself one point for a fly, two points for a beetle, four points for a wasp, and a million points for an elephant. Ketchup-Face, meanwhile, sat at the front of the basket, making horsey noises and shouting things like,

'Giddy-up!'

'I shall call you Starlight,' she said to the shopping trolley.

'Actually,' said the shopping trolley, 'my name's Eric.'

Ketchup-Face was the sort of child who never let facts get in the way of a good game. 'Giddy-up, Starlight!' she said, and added to Stinkbomb, 'Well, we've met a cat who gave us a shoe, and a horsey who gave us a ride . . . '

'I'm not a horsey,' the shopping trolley pointed out.

' . . . so I wonder who we'll meet next?'

'A million!' answered Stinkbomb happily, pulling something out of his mouth and examining it. 'I've caught an elephant!'

'Don't worry, elephant,' said Ketchup-Face.

'Stinkbomb has bravely saved you from his own mouth. Now you can give us something magical to help us on our quest.' Then she looked closer. 'Wait a minute,' she said. 'That's not an elephant. It's a beetle with a big nose.'

The elephant, if that's what it was, made a little **buzzing** noise and flew away.

Some time later, the little shopping trolley drew to a halt.

'I can take you no further,' it said sadly, 'for we have reached the enchanted wood where the badgers dwell.'

Stinkbomb and Ketchup-Face looked, but they could see no wood before them.

'Gosh!' said Stinkbomb. 'It really is enchanted, isn't it? It's invisible!'

'Erm, no,' said the little shopping trolley; 'you're just facing the wrong way.'

'Oh,' said Stinkbomb and Ketchup-Face together. They turned round; and there, dark and forbidding, stood the enchanted wood.

'You must carry on alone,' the shopping trolley continued, 'for the bracken and brambles are too thick for my little wheels to get through. Besides which, I promised my mum I'd tidy my room this afternoon. But if you ever need help, call me and I shall answer. Unless I'm busy, or too far away to hear, or watching a good programme on telly or something. Farewell, Stinkbomb and Ketchup-Face!'

'Farewell, Starlight, my noble steed!' said Ketchup-Face, trying to fling her arms around the little shopping trolley's neck, but then realizing it didn't have one, and settling for patting it on the handle instead.

'Yeah, bye, shopping trolley,' said Stinkbomb. 'Thanks for the lift.'

They waved goodbye until the little shopping trolley was out of sight, and then turned and began to walk into the wood.

chapter 9

In which our heroes walk into the wood and have a strange encounter

'It's a bit scary, isn't it?' Ketchup-Face said after a while.

Stinkbomb reached out to her. 'You can hold my hand if it makes you feel better,' he said.

'Oof!'

he added, as he fell over. 'That's not my hand;
it's my foot.'

'Sorry,' said Ketchup-Face. 'It's a bit dark and
gloomy in here. Have you got a torch?'

'I think so,' said Stinkbomb, picking himself
up and rummaging in his pockets. 'Yes—
here's one.' He pulled it out and tried to switch
it on, but it turned out to be a Cornish pasty,
so he ate it. Then he tried again, and eventually
produced a small torch shaped like a squirrel
in a bow tie, which played *The Wheels on the
Bus* when he pushed the switch. It gave out
only a very dim light, but it was better than
nothing.

They set off through the wood. The thick bracken and tangled brambles made it hard going, and the dim beam from the torch flickered about, casting strange shadows.

After a while, Ketchup-Face said, 'Why's the torchlight so wobbly and all shaking around?'

'Because I can't hold it steady,' explained Stink-bomb.

'Why not?' asked Ketchup-Face.

'Because I'm **hopping**,' Stinkbomb said.

'Oh,' said Ketchup-Face. 'Why are you **hopping**? You've got two shoes on.'

'Yes,' said Stinkbomb, 'but you're still holding my foot.'

'Oh, OK,' said Ketchup-Face. 'I wonder if we're going to meet someone else soon who can help us find the badgers.'

Stinkbomb shrugged. 'Another animal, you mean?' he said. 'There are probably loads of animals in here.'

'Yes, but actually, it might not be an animal this time,' said Ketchup-Face, who considered herself something of an expert on stories. 'It might be a strange little man. In loads of old stories, when the heroes are on a quest, it gets to a bit where they need help, and then they meet someone who's going to help them, and it says something like, "Just then, they met the strangest little man they had ever seen."'

Just then, they met the strangest little man they had ever seen. He had bright, beady little eyes, and little round ears, and a pointy triangular face, and he was covered in thick grey and black fur—except for his head, which was white with two broad black stripes running from nose to neck. His legs were short and stumpy, and he had four of them, one at each corner.

Oh, and he had a fat stubby little tail, and his breath smelt of worms and dustbins, and he was standing in a clearing spray-painting the words BADGERS RULE on a tree.

'Hello, strange little man,' said Ketchup-Face cheerily. 'Are you going to help us on our quest?'

'Depends,' said the strange little man, jumping guiltily and hiding his spray can. 'What kind of quest is it?'

'Well,' said Ketchup-Face,

'I am Ketchup-Face and this is Stinkbomb, and we have been sent by the King to rid the kingdom of all **badgers!**'

'Yes,' said Stinkbomb, 'but we need to find them first.'

The strange little man's beady little eyes narrowed, becoming even more beady and even more little. 'Is that so?' he said. 'And why would you want to get rid of the badgers?'

'Because we have found out all about their **evil** and **wicked** doings,' said Ketchup-Face, who had a strong sense of the dramatic.

'What,' said the strange little man, his sharp little face looking suddenly worried, '**all** about their evil and wicked doings?'

'Oh, yes,' said Ketchup-Face. 'Or at least, all about all the evil and wicked doings we've found out about. I suppose they might have done others.'

'I see,' said the strange little man thoughtfully.

'So,' said Stinkbomb, 'Can you take us to the place where the badgers live? It's by a magical stream, just next to a small block of flats.'

'Um, not sure,' said the strange little man thoughtfully. 'But I've got lots of mates, and some of them might be able to help. Just wait here— I'll be back in a few minutes.'

And, dropping his spray can, he disappeared into the undergrowth.

Stinkbomb and Ketchup-Face waited.

After a bit, Stinkbomb said, 'Ketchup-Face?'

'Yes?' said Ketchup-Face.

'Do you think you could let go of my foot now?'

'Um, OK,' said Ketchup-Face, and she did.

After another minute or two, Ketchup-Face said, 'Stinkbomb?'

'Yes?' said Stinkbomb.

'Why do chapters always have to end just when something's happening?'

'What do you mean?' asked Stinkbomb.

'Well,' said Ketchup-Face, 'like when we got to the palace, or when King Toothbrush Weasel went upstairs to get dressed. It's always when something's happening. They never end when you're just standing around waiting or something like that.'

'They could do, though,' said Stinkbomb.

'Could they?'

'Yeah,' said Stinkbomb knowledgeably. 'Chapters can end whenever they like. They could even end in the middle of a

In which Stinkbomb finishes his sentence, and our heroes find themselves in terrible danger

sentence, if they wanted to.'

'Gosh!' said Ketchup-Face, impressed.

Just then, the strange little man reappeared.

'Hello again, strange little man,' said Ketchup-Face brightly.

'Er, yeah, hello,' the strange little man said gruffly. 'I've brought lots of other strange little men. Maybe one of them can help you.'

And, suddenly, the clearing was full of strange little men, all of them looking very like the first, and most of them with rather unpleasant expressions on their pointy, stripey, furry faces.

'Hello, strange little men!' said Ketchup-Face.

'Right, all you other, um, strange little men,' said the first strange little man meaningfully. 'These two are here because they've found out about all the badgers' **evil** and **wicked** doings what they've been doing **evilly** and **wickedly**. So we're going to, um, help them find the badgers.'

There was a muttering from amongst the strange little men, and they **shuffled** forwards in a way that Stinkbomb and Ketchup-Face did not find

altogether comfort-
able. And then one
of them—a particu-
larly small strange
little man with a high
squeaky voice—said, in a puzzled tone:

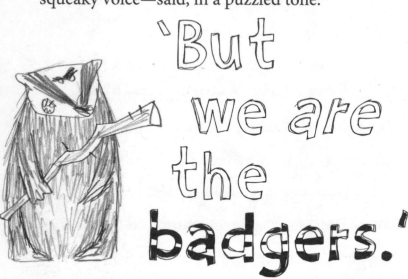

'But we are the badgers.'

'Shhh! Shut up, Stewart the Badger!'

hissed all the other badgers, for that is what they were. But it was too late; Stink-bomb and Ketchup-Face had heard.

Ketchup-Face's eyes narrowed. 'You never said you were badgers,' she said accusingly.

'Er, we're not,' said one of the badgers. 'We're, er, lemmings. Isn't that right, Rolf the Badger?'

'That's right,' agreed Rolf the Badger, a big badger with a big badge that said (Big Badger). 'We're not badgers at all. Are we, Harry the Badger?'

'No,' agreed Harry the Badger, taking a sip of tea from a mug marked, World's Best Badger. 'We're not even slightly badgery. Are we, Stewart the Badger?'

'Yes, we are,' said Stewart the Badger cheerfully. Harry the Badger passed him a note that said:

Pretend you're not a badger.

Stewart the Badger read it slowly three times and then added, 'Er, no, we're not.' He turned the note over. On the other side it said:

Pretend you're a lemming.

'Er, I'm a lemming,' he added.

Ketchup-Face smiled a relieved sort of smile. 'Oh, well, that's all right, then,' she said. 'Can you tell us where to find the badgers?'

But Stinkbomb was not so easily fooled. He reached into his pocket and pulled out a book he had borrowed from King Toothbrush Weasel. It was called *The Wrong Book*, but it was the wrong book, so he put it back and pulled out another one called *How to Identify a Badger*. He leafed through it quickly, noting the badgers' stripey heads, grey and black fur, and thick, muscular bodies. 'Are you *sure* you're not badgers?' he asked suspiciously.

'Oh, yes,' said all the badgers. 'Quite sure.'

Stinkbomb turned to the chapter entitled *Absolutely Foolproof Ways to Identify a Badger*, read it carefully, and then reached into his pocket and pulled out a dustbin, a chicken, and a sports car.

Immediately, the badgers knocked over the dustbin, frightened the chicken, and drove the sports car too fast.

Stinkbomb's eyes widened as he realized the danger they were in.

'It's the badgers!'

he yelled.

'Run!'

'OK,' said Ketchup-Face, sitting down.

'Can you help me with the laces?

Oof!'

she added, as she disappeared under a pile of badgers.

Stinkbomb was outraged.

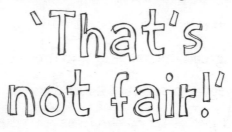

'That's not fair!'

he said.

Rolf the Badger looked up from his position on top of the pile. 'Isn't it?' he said.

'No, it's not!' said Stinkbomb firmly. 'She hadn't finished putting her shoe on. It's cheating to jump on her before she's ready.'

The badgers blushed. 'Sorry,' they mumbled, and got off Ketchup-Face. Stewart the Badger even helped her with her shoelace, just to make amends.

'Right,' said Stinkbomb. 'Now you have to give us a head start.'

'OK,' agreed the badgers, and they closed their eyes and began to count to a hundred.

They'd got as far as thirty-seven when Harry the Badger opened his eyes and said, 'Hang on! We're not *supposed* to be fair! We're the bad guys!'

All the other badgers took their paws away from their faces and said, 'Oh, *yeah!* I forgot!'— all, that is, except Stewart the Badger, who said, '*Are* we? Awwww!'

'Get them!'

cried Rolf the Badger.

'Er . . . get who?' asked Stewart the Badger, looking round, puzzled.

'Those pesky kids, of course!' growled Harry the Badger.

But there was no sign of Stinkbomb and Ketchup-Face.

growled Harry the Badger in an especially growly way, just to prove he was a bad guy. 'After them!'

'But we don't know which way they've gone,' Stewart the Badger pointed out. Rolf the Badger kicked him on the bottom, because he wanted to prove he was a bad guy as well. All the other badgers laughed, not because it was particularly funny, but just because they were bad guys too.

Harry the Badger sighed a **big** sigh, 'We're animals, right?' he said. 'So we can track 'em down using our animal senses.'

'Right,' said Stewart the Badger eagerly. 'So . . . we should try **touching** them until we find them!'

Rolf the Badger gave him a hard stare. 'How're you going to **touch** them before you've found them?'

Stewart the Badger scratched his head. 'I see what you mean,' he said. 'So . . . we should try **tasting** them until we find them?'

Harry the Badger clipped him round the ear. 'We've got five senses, Stewart the Badger,' he said. 'Trust you to pick the wrong two for tracking.'

'Oh,' said Stewart the Badger. 'Right. Well ...'
He looked all around the clearing, but he couldn't
see either Stinkbomb or Ketchup-Face, for the
very simple reason that they weren't there. Then
he tried **smelling** them, but he couldn't smell
anything except for the perfumed blossom of the
woodland trees, the sweet smell of the woodland
flowers, and the **stinky stink** of the woodland
rubbish that had spilled out when they knocked
the bin over.

So then he **listened** very, very hard; and
so did all the other badgers; and after a while,
they **heard** something. In fact, they **heard** two
somethings.

'Listen!' said Rolf the Badger. 'Is it me, or does one of them noises sound like a frightened chicken?'

'Yeah,' agreed Harry the Badger, 'and the other one sounds like a squirrel with a bow tie playing *The Wheels on the Bus*.'

'After them!' cried all the other badgers except Stewart the Badger.

'But it sounds like they're miles away,' Stewart the Badger pointed out. 'We'll never catch them now.'

'Oh, yes we will,' said Harry the Badger. 'Because you, Stewart the Badger, have failed to notice one very important thing.'

'What's that?' asked Stewart the Badger.

'They've left their sports car behind!' said Harry the Badger. 'Come on!'

And all the badgers jumped into the sports

car and roared out of the clearing, driving much too fast, and knocking the dustbin over again as they left.

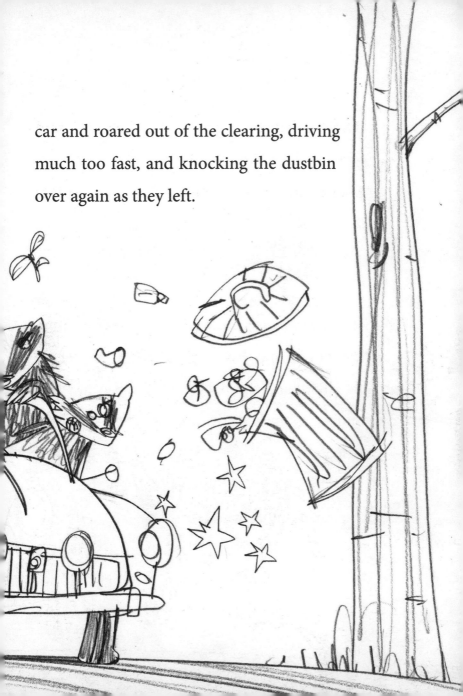

chapter 11

Then there was a chase, which was really exciting. Stinkbomb and Ketchup-Face ran as quickly as they could, and the badgers drove too fast and caught up with them, and Stinkbomb and Ketchup-Face tried running even faster, but they couldn't, and the chicken got really really frightened and stuck its head out of Stinkbomb's pocket and went Buk-AWWWWK! and then the badgers caught them. Except for the chicken, which jumped out of Stinkbomb's pocket and ran away.

All right, so it doesn't look quite so exciting written down; but it was.

Buk-Awwwwk.!

Anyway, then the badgers picked Stinkbomb and Ketchup-Face up and put them in the car.

'Help! Help!'

shouted Stinkbomb and Ketchup-Face; but there was no answer. Then they shouted,

'Hemmmmph! Mmmmph!'

because the badgers had thrown them on to the back seat of the car and sat on their faces.

Then the badgers drove back to the clearing where they lived, and carried Stinkbomb and Ketchup-Face into the crumbling block of flats next to their home. There, in a little basement room with horrid brown and mustard-yellow swirly carpet on the walls and orange wallpaper on the floor, the children learned the dreadful fate that was to be theirs.

'Right,' said Harry the Badger. 'We can't have you two goin' around telling everyone about our **evil** and **wicked** doings.'

'No,' said Stewart the Badger. 'Especially the one where we're going to get rid of King Toothbrush Weasel and replace him with King Harry the Badger.'

'Oh,' said Ketchup-Face. 'We didn't know about that one.'

'Didn't you?' said Stewart the Badger, surprised. 'What about the one where we're going to take all the mums in Great Kerfuffle prisoner and force them to make us packed lunches every day?'

'Yeah,' agreed Rolf the Badger, 'with **worm sandwiches** and **dustbin sauce**!'

'Mmmm! Yum!' said all the other badgers.

'Nope,' said Stinkbomb. 'We didn't know about that one either.'

'What about,' said Stewart the Badger, 'the one where we're going to put saddles on all the dads and make them give us piggy backs everywhere?'

Stinkbomb and Ketchup-Face shook their heads.

'Oh,' said Stewart the Badger. 'Maybe we should let them go. It doesn't look like they *do* know about our evil and wicked doings after all.'

Harry the Badger clipped him round the ear again. 'Except that you've just told them, haven't you? So now there's nothing else for it. Rolf the Badger: fetch ... the box!'

Rolf the Badger fetched a box. It was a big cardboard box.

'Right,' said Harry the Badger. 'Now for another **evil** and **wicked** doing.' He laughed a **wicked** laugh, and then passed round a box marked Evil Moustaches, and each badger took one and twirled it **evilly**. 'What we're going to do is,' Harry the Badger went on, 'we're going to put you in this box, and then we're going to post you to the remote mountain kingdom of Bajerstan where you'll be put to work painting stripes on second-hand tigers.'

Stinkbomb thought about this. The idea of being put in a cardboard box and posted to the remote mountain kingdom of Bajerstan and then being put to work painting **stripes** on second-hand tigers certainly sounded interesting, but on balance he wasn't sure if he fancied it.

Ketchup-Face, on the other hand, was most indignant. 'You can't put me in a box and post me to the remote mountain kingdom of Bajerstan and make me paint **stripes** on second-hand tigers!' she protested. 'What about my fans?'

'What fans?' demanded Rolf the Badger.

Ketchup-Face straightened in a most dignified manner. 'When I'm grown up,' she said, 'I'm going to be a famous singer, and people will come from miles around to see me, and if I'm not there 'cos I'm painting **stripes** on second-hand tigers in the remote mountain kingdom of Bajerstan, they're going to be all disappointed.'

'Oh,' said Harry the Badger. 'That's a shame. Oh, well, never mind.'

'Never mind?' said Ketchup-Face. '*Never mind?*'

'Um . . . maybe she could sing a song for us now?' suggested Stewart the Badger, who liked songs, and was aware that we hadn't had one since Chapter Two.

'Good idea, Stewart the Badger!' exclaimed Harry the Badger.

'Is it?' asked Stewart the Badger in surprise. He wasn't used to having good ideas.

'Not really,' admitted Harry the Badger. 'It's probably a stupid idea; but let's do it anyway. All right, little girl: what are you going to sing for us?'

Ketchup-Face cleared her throat. 'I'm going to sing a song which is a work of complete genius,' she said. 'It's quite probably the best song in the world, and it's called *Blueberry Jam*.'

chapter 12

In which Ketchup-Face sings

'Blueberry jam,' sang Ketchup-Face.
'Blueberry jam

Blueberry jam, blueberry jam

Blueberry, blueberry, blueberry jam

Bluey, bluey, bluey, bluey

Bluey, bluey, blueberry jam

Blueberry jam

Blueberry *jam*

The badgers applauded politely.

'Well done,' said Harry the Badger. 'Right—into the box you go.'

Ketchup-Face fixed him with a steely glare. 'I haven't finished yet,' she said. 'That was just the first verse.'

'Oh—sorry,' said Harry the Badger. 'I thought there only was one.'

'I wrote some more,' said Ketchup-Face, with a touch of pride. ''Cos the first verse was so good, only it needed more jam.'

And she cleared her throat once more, and began to sing the second verse.

chapter 13

In which Ketchup-Face sings the second verse

'Raspberry jam,' sang Ketchup-Face.

'Raspberry jam

Raspberry jam, raspberry jam

Raspberry, raspberry, raspberry jam

Raspy, raspy, raspy, raspy

Raspy, raspy, raspberry jam

Raspberry jam

Raspberry *jam*

The badgers were about to put their paws together when Ketchup-Face fixed them with another steely glare.

'There's more?' enquired Harry the Badger hesitantly.

Ketchup-Face nodded, and began to sing the next verse.

chapter 14

In which Ketchup-Face sings the third verse

The third verse was about gooseberry jam.

This time, Ketchup-Face got the steely glare in before the badgers had time to applaud. Then she continued.

chapter 15

The twenty-seventh verse was about redcurrant jam.

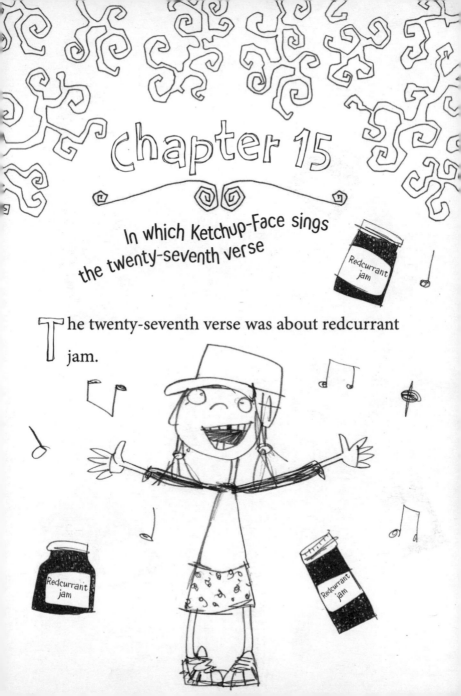

The fifty-third verse was about cauliflower jam.

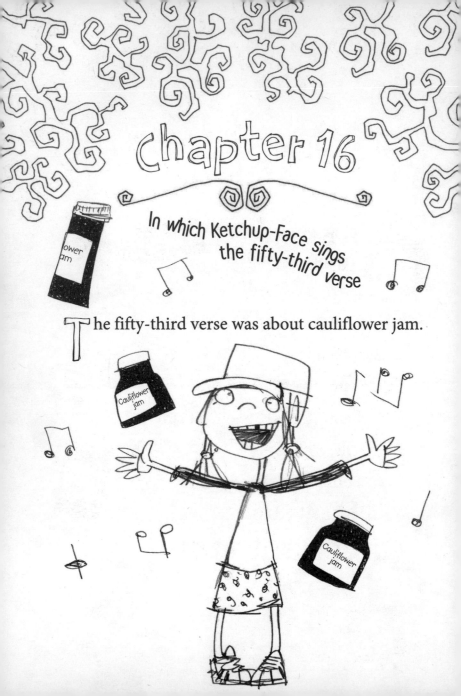

chapter 17

In which Ketchup-Face sings
the seven hundred and eightieth verse

'Elephant jam,' sang Ketchup-Face.

'Elephant jam

Elephant jam, elephant jam

Elephant, elephant, elephant jam

Elly, elly, elly, elly

Elly, elly, elephant jam

Elephant jam

Elephant *jam*

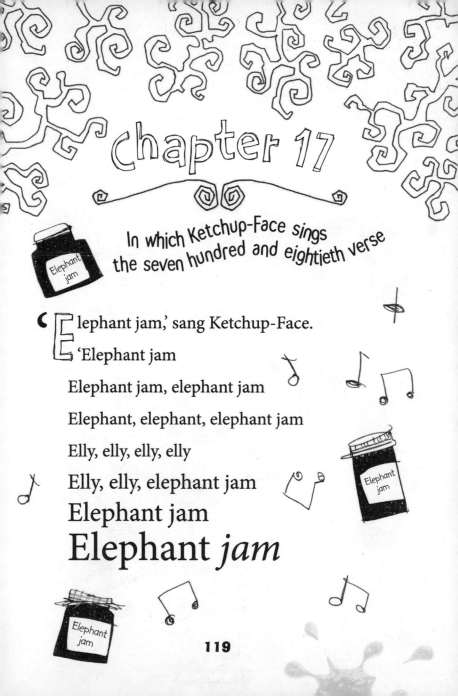

Stewart the Badger yawned, and Ketchup-Face fixed him with another steely glare. This was the five hundred and third steely glare she'd fixed a badger with since the song began, and she felt she was getting rather good at it.

'Did you say something?' she enquired coldly.

'Um, no, not at all,' Stewart the Badger said miserably. Somewhere around the two hundred and fiftieth verse—the one beginning 'Daffodil jam'—the other badgers had sneaked off, leaving him in charge, with strict instructions to call them when Ketchup-Face had finished her song. Unfortunately, this didn't seem to be about to happen.

chapter 18

In which Ketchup-Face sings
the four thousand, seven hundred
and sixty-ninth verse

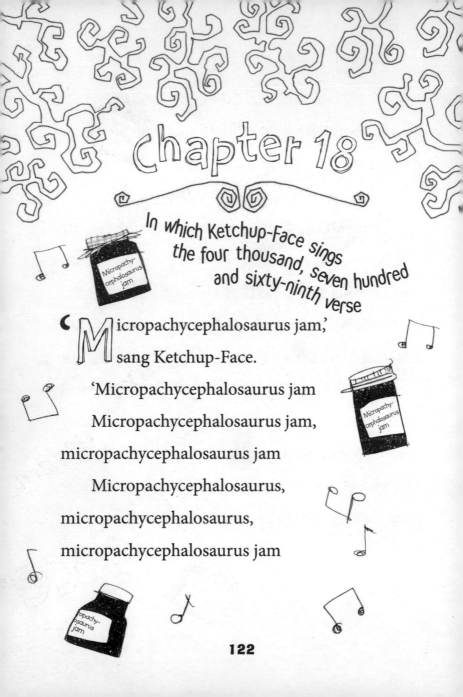

'Micropachycephalosaurus jam,'
sang Ketchup-Face.

'Micropachycephalosaurus jam

Micropachycephalosaurus jam,

micropachycephalosaurus jam

Micropachycephalosaurus,

micropachycephalosaurus,

micropachycephalosaurus jam

122

Micro, micro, micro, micro

Micro, micro, micropachycephalosaurus jam

Micropachycephalosaurus jam

Micropachycephalosaurus jam

Micropachycephalosaurus jam

Micropachyce

She fixed Stewart the Badger with another steely
glare as he got up.

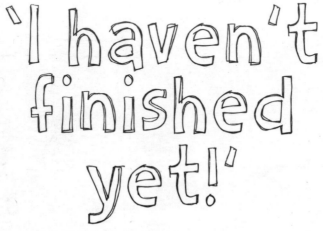

she said. 'And all the other badgers have sneaked
off. You have to stay and be my audience.'

'Um, feel free to carry on without me,' said Stewart the Badger, wriggling uncomfortably. 'I'll be back
in a minute. It's just that, um, I need to go for a poo.'

And he made a dash for the door.

'Quick!' said Stinkbomb. 'Let's get out of here!'

Ketchup-Face fixed him with a steely glare. 'I haven't finished my song!' she said.

'You can finish it later,' Stinkbomb told her.

'But I'm nearly at the best bit!'

'Look,' Stinkbomb said, 'either you can finish the song now—and then the badgers will put us in a cardboard box and post us to the remote mountain kingdom of Bajerstan where we'll be put to work painting **stripes** on second-hand tigers—or we can escape and go home, and then you can sing your song to Mum and Dad after the end of the story.'

Ketchup-Face thought about this. 'Mum and Dad would probably like my song, wouldn't they?' she said.

Stinkbomb nodded. 'I expect they'd love it.'

'What about the second-hand tigers?' Ketchup-Face asked. 'They'd like it too, wouldn't they?'

Stinkbomb shook his head. 'Probably not,' he said.

'Oh,' said Ketchup-Face. 'Are you sure?'

'Pretty sure,' Stinkbomb said.

'Tigers have rubbish taste in music.'

'Oh, OK,' Ketchup-Face said. 'I wouldn't want the tigers to be disappointed, that's all. Time to escape, then!'

And they escaped.

Or, at least, they did the first bit of escaping, which involved tiptoeing to the lift. The lift was broken, but Ketchup-Face fixed it with a steely glare, and they got in and went up to the ground floor and tiptoed out the front door. Unfortunately, as soon as they had done that, they found themselves entirely surrounded by badgers.

'Oi!' said Harry the Badger gruffly. 'What're you doing escaping, when you should be finishing your song and getting into a box?'

'Yeah!' agreed Rolf the Badger. 'And what've you done with Stewart the Badger?'

'I'll be down in a minute,' came a high squeaky voice from an upstairs window. 'I'm just wiping my bottom.'

The badgers growled. They were in a very bad mood by this point, because not only had most of them not had anything to say yet; it looked as if—apart from Stewart the Badger, and Rolf the Badger, and Harry the Badger—none of them was even going to be given a name before the end of the story. They closed in on our heroes, and it looked as if this time there was no way out. But then . . .

'What's that squeaking noise?' said Ketchup-Face.

The badgers turned and saw a horrifying

World's
Best
Badger

sight, except that it wasn't very horrifying. But it was definitely a sight, and they saw it. Coming towards them—most of the time, except when it veered off to one side—was the little shopping trolley; and sitting proudly upright in the little shopping trolley was King Toothbrush Weasel; and sitting on King Toothbrush Weasel's head, nesting in the centre of his crown, was the frightened chicken.

'I say!' said King Toothbrush Weasel, as the little shopping trolley drew near and steered sideways into a tree. 'What are you two doing here in the middle of all these antelopes?'

'They're not antelopes, they're badgers,' said Stinkbomb, opening *How to Identify a Badger* at a picture of a badger and handing it to King Tooth-brush Weasel.

'Oh, yes,' said King Toothbrush Weasel, looking at the picture. 'So they are. The octopus told me you were in trouble, so we've come to help.'

'What octopus?' said Ketchup-Face.

'This one, of course,' said King Toothbrush Weasel, pointing at the frightened chicken. 'Well— it didn't exactly tell me, but it did a mime and drew a picture.'

'And I heard your cries for help,' said the little shopping trolley, 'and my mum said my room was nearly tidy and I'd worked very hard and I could finish it later; so I came too. And luckily someone's been driving a sports car too fast in the enchanted wood, and they've **squashed** all the brambles and bracken down so I can get in now.'

`Buk-AWWWWWWK!'

added the frightened chicken; and the badgers started muttering darkly, for many of them felt it wasn't fair that even a frightened chicken should get to say more than them.

'Here I am,' said Stewart the Badger, bursting through the doors behind Stinkbomb and Ketch-up-Face. 'Have I missed anything?'

Rolf the Badger looked at him suspiciously. 'Did you wash your paws?' he asked.

Stewart the Badger blushed. 'Whoops!' he said, and disappeared again.

'So now,' continued King Toothbrush Weasel, 'I shall rescue you from these **wicked** . . . ' —here he paused and checked the book again—'badgers.'

'Oh, yeah?' said Harry the Badger. 'You and whose army?'

'Me and *my* army, of course!' said King Toothbrush Weasel.

said the army, emerging from behind him and springing gracefully up on to the edge of the basket.

'Oooooooh,'

murmured the badgers nervously.

They'd never seen a whole army before.

'Right!'

said Malcolm the Cat.

'You're all under arrest.'

'Are we really?' asked Rolf the Badger.

'No, not really,' said Malcolm the Cat. 'You can all go, as long as you promise not to do it again. OK?'

The badgers nodded, and began to shuffle away.

'Oh, hold on a minute,' Malcolm the Cat said. 'My mistake. You *are* under arrest after all.'

'Awww,' said the badgers, and they all came and stood in front of Malcolm the Cat and waited to be handcuffed.

'Although,' said Malcolm the Cat, 'I suppose if you were very good, I could let you go ...' And then, as the badgers began to shuffle hopefully away again, he added, 'Or maybe not.'

The doors to the block of flats opened again, and Stewart the Badger emerged once more. 'Have I missed anything?' he asked.

'Yeah,' said Harry the Badger glumly. 'We're all being arrested by the army.'

Stewart the Badger looked at the army. 'But it's only a cat,' he said.

'Oh, yeah,' said all the badgers. 'So it is.'

And they grabbed Stinkbomb and Ketchup-Face, and King Toothbrush Weasel, and Malcolm the Cat, and the little shopping trolley, and the frightened chicken, and put them in the cardboard box and posted them to the remote mountain kingdom of Bajerstan.

chapter 20

In which our heroes get bored in a cardboard box

It was very cramped in the box. Stinkbomb ended up with King Toothbrush Weasel's elbow up his nose and Malcolm the Cat's tail in his ear; and the frightened chicken laid an egg on his head.

'Hey!' said Ketchup-Face, from her folded-up position underneath the little shopping trolley. 'I can get my toes in my mouth!'

Stinkbomb had a go, and found that he could get his toes in his mouth as well, which was at least something to do to pass the time. They discovered that they could get their toes in each other's mouths, too; but King Toothbrush Weasel wouldn't let them try to get their toes in his mouth because he said that sort of thing wasn't very royal.

When that got boring, they had a game of **I Spy** which wasn't much fun because the badgers had taken Stinkbomb's torch, so everyone's go began 'I spy with my little eye something beginning with **D**,' and then everyone else guessed Darkness and was right every time—except when it was Ketchup-Face's go. Her **D** turned out to be for **D**oris, who she said was her imaginary friend. This made Stinkbomb a bit cross because he knew Ketchup-Face's imaginary friend was called Salary, which didn't begin with **D**, even the way Ketchup-Face spelled it.

'Anyway,' he complained. 'How can you see her in the dark?'

'Because she's imaginary,' Ketchup-Face explained.

Fairly soon they stopped playing that, and Stinkbomb and Ketchup-Face took it in turns to say 'Are we nearly there yet?' every five minutes.

And all the time, the box was **bumping** and **jolting** and doing all those things that boxes do when they're in the post.

At last, they felt the box being put down, and there was the unmistakable sound of a door being knocked.

'Is this the second-hand tiger factory?' asked Ketchup-Face. 'I can't hear any tigers.'

A moment later, the unmistakable sound of a door being knocked came again. Then there was the unmistakable sound of a postman filling out one of those 'Sorry you were out when I called' cards and posting it through a letterbox, and then the unmistakable feeling of being carried round to be left behind a bin at the back of the house. And then came the unmistakable sound of a postman driving away, followed by the unmistakable sound of nothing happening.

After a bit, Ketchup-Face said, 'I'm bored of being in this box. Can we get out now?'

'I'm afraid we're still trapped in here,' King Toothbrush Weasel told her. 'If someone doesn't come and let us out, we could be stuck in this box until it rains enough to make the cardboard go all soggy and mushy.'

Stinkbomb thought about this. The idea of being stuck in a box until it rained enough to make the cardboard go all **soggy** and **mushy** certainly sounded interesting, but on balance he wasn't sure if he fancied it.

'If only we had a knife,' said the little shopping trolley, vainly bashing its basket against the side of the box in a futile attempt to escape.

'But I do!' said Stinkbomb in great excitement, suddenly remembering. Wriggling his hand round, he managed to reach into his pocket; and after pulling out a **comic**,

a **bag of crisps**,

a **cardboard elephant**,

a **telegraph pole**,

an **interestingly-shaped rock**,

and a **squirrel**,

he eventually produced a shiny and very sharp **penknife**, with which he cut a door in the wall of the box.

chapter 21

In which our heroes escape from the cardboard box, and Ketchup-Face makes a discovery

'We're free!' shouted the little shopping trolley.

'Hurrah!' yelled King Toothbrush Weasel.

'Buk-AWWWWWK!' said the frightened chicken.

Malcolm the Cat had gone to sleep in the little shopping trolley's basket during the game of **I Spy**, so he didn't say anything; and neither did Stinkbomb, who just looked pleased with himself. But Ketchup-Face was eyeing the penknife **suspiciously**.

'Is that new?' she asked.

Stinkbomb nodded. 'I bought it yesterday,' he said. 'I've been wanting one for ages.'

'Where did you get the money for it?' Ketchup-Face said.

Stinkbomb rolled his eyes impatiently. 'If you *must* know,' he said, 'I had a tenner in my piggy bank, and I . . . '

And then he stopped.

'Oh,' he said.

He went red.

'Oh,' he said again.

And then he said, `Ow!' because Ketchup-Face was jumping **up** and **down** on his toes.

'You *idiot*, Stinkbomb!'

she was yelling.

'You useless pile of dandruff! You enormous cabbagey cushion! You stupid frog-flavoured envelope!'

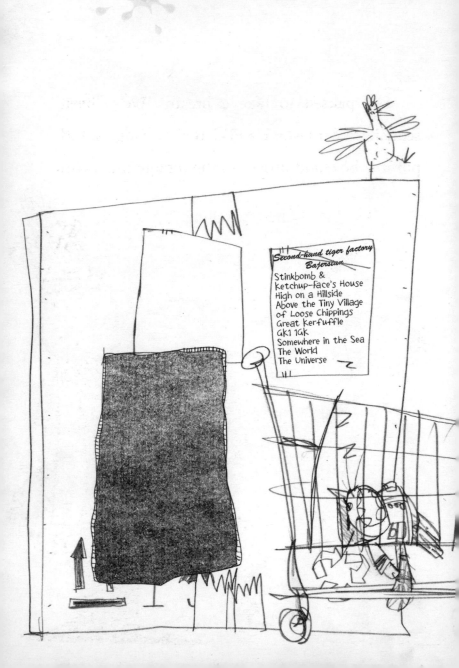

Second-hand tiger factory
Bajersum

Stinkbomb &
Ketchup-face's House
High on a Hillside
Above the Tiny Village
of Loose Chippings
Great Kerfuffle
GK1 1GK
Somewhere in the Sea
The World
The Universe

She paused to take a breath. 'We've been scared in a dark wood, and chased by badgers, and put in a box, and posted to the remote mountain

You useless pile of dandruff!

King

kingdom of Bajerstan to paint **stripes** on second-hand tigers for the rest of our lives, and I didn't even get to finish my song, and now it turns out the badgers didn't even steal your tenner at all, not even a little bit! It's all your fault!'

King Toothbrush Weasel was suddenly looking very serious. 'You mean the badgers aren't **evil** and **wicked** after all?' he said. 'Oh, dear. Poor innocent creatures. We have misjudged them.'

'Well, not—OW—really,' explained Stink-bomb. 'I mean, they did—OW—put us in a box and post us to the—OW—remote mountain kingdom of Bajer—OW—stan.'

'Yes,' added Ketchup-Face breathlessly, still

jumping. 'And they're going to force all the mummies to make their horrid packed lunches, and make all the daddies give them piggy-back rides.'

'That's right,' said Stinkbomb; 'and—OW—they're going to replace you with—OW—King Harry the Badger. OW.'

'OW,' agreed Ketchup-Face, as she fell over, exhausted, to lie panting on the grass.

'What?' said King Toothbrush Weasel, **horror-struck**. 'Overthrow me and put a badger on the throne of Great Kerfuffle? But . . . but that's treacle!'

'Um, I think you mean *treason*, your Majesty,' said the little shopping trolley shyly.

'Nonsense!' said King Toothbrush Weasel.

'Treason is sort of like runny toffee. Anyway, we have to stop them!'

'But how?' asked Ketchup-Face. 'We're in the remote mountain kingdom of Bajerstan.'

'Er, no we're not,' said the little shopping trolley.

They looked around, and found it was true.

'Well, bless my soul,' said King Toothbrush Weasel, 'how did we get here?'

It was like a miracle, or at least like one of those times when the postman delivers a parcel to the wrong house. Far from being in the remote mountain kingdom of Bajerstan, they were behind a bin round the back of Stinkbomb's and Ketchup-Face's very own home, on a hillside above the tiny village of Loose Chippings.

The little shopping trolley was examining the box. 'Look!' it said. 'Someone's changed the address!'

Stinkbomb looked. 'Oh, yeah,' he said. 'I forgot I'd done that.'

'*You* did this?' asked King Toothbrush Weasel.

Stinkbomb nodded. 'Yeah,' he said. 'While Ketchup-Face was singing her song. During the verse about duck-billed platypus jam. I got a bit bored, so I got out a pen and wrote my name and address on the box.'

'And a good thing, too!' said King Toothbrush Weasel. 'But how will we stop the badgers doing any more **evil** and **wicked** doings?'

They all went

'Hmmm,'

and scratched their heads for a bit.

Then Stinkbomb jumped up and pointed at the dustbin. 'That bin has given me an idea!' he said. 'But we'll have to be really quick!'

'Why?' asked King Toothbrush Weasel worriedly.

'Because we're almost at the end of the story,' explained Ketchup-Face.

'And we need to get to a shop,' added Stinkbomb.

'Quickly, Starlight, my noble steed!'

shouted Ketchup-Face.

'Who?' said the little shopping trolley. 'Oh—oh, right.'

'Ow!' said Malcolm the Cat, waking up as Ketchup-Face jumped into the basket and sat on him. 'Ow! Ow!' he added, as Stinkbomb and King Toothbrush Weasel and the frightened chicken scrambled in after her.

'Where to?' asked the little shopping trolley eagerly.

'Full speed ahead!'

yelled Stinkbomb.

'To the village of

Loose Chippings!'

chapter 22

In which the badgers get what's coming to them, and all ends happily

As soon as the sun had set, the badgers crept out of the enchanted wood and stole across the valley. **A-snuffling** and **a-scurrying** they came, their teeth and claws all gleaming and badgery in the moonlight. Their hearts were filled with **evil** and **wickedness**, and their minds were filled with thoughts of treason, and their tummies were filled with worms and bits of rubbish.

The other creatures sensed with their animal senses that the badgers were on the move, and they were filled with fear. The cows cowered, and the quails quailed, and the foxes lay in bed recovering from having been **squashed** by the pigs. Some of the braver animals made their feelings clear as the badgers passed by—a snake **hissed**; a snail **booed**; a blackbird blew a **raspberry**; a raspbird blew a **blackberry**; a hedgehog wrote a **cross letter** to the newspapers—but mostly they just hid, knowing that whatever the badgers were up to, they were up to no good.

But as the badgers, intent on **evil**, came over the hill and entered the valley that led down to the tiny village of Loose Chippings, they saw a marvellous sight such as they had never seen before.

It was a trail of dustbins, all of them **shiny** and **new**, leading right through the village and just begging to be **knocked over**.

'Yes!'

shouted the badgers; and they were just about to rush forward and knock all the bins over when Harry the Badger spoke.

'Hang about!' he said, in a voice so commanding that the badgers all immediately hung about. 'We can't go knocking all these bins over!'

'But ... but we're badgers!' said Stewart the Badger.

'Yeah!' agreed Rolf the Badger. 'What kind of badgers would we be if we went about not knocking bins over?'

Harry the Badger folded his paws and looked sternly at them. 'Quiet badgers, that's what kind,' he said. 'We're supposed to be being quiet so we can get to the palace under cover of darkness and make me king!'

'Yeah,' said Rolf the Badger, 'but we could just knock over a few bins on the way, couldn't we?'

'*Pleee-ase!*' added Stewart the Badger; and all the other badgers put their paws together, stuck their bottom lips out, and made their eyes really really big, because they'd once heard from a little girl that it's a good way to get what you want.

'No!' said Harry the Badger sternly.

'*AWWWWW!*'

said all the badgers.

'Well,' said Harry the Badger, 'maybe just the one. As long as you're very, very quiet.'

'Hurray!'

whispered all the badgers; and they set off again. They were as silent as they could be, although Stewart the Badger kept whistling under his breath because the tune to *Blueberry Jam* was stuck in his head. It wasn't a terribly catchy tune, but he had heard it four thousand, seven hundred and sixty-nine times. Rolf the Badger had to keep nudging him to be quiet.

Into the village the badgers tiptoed, agog with wonder at the number and variety of bins on offer. Which one should they knock over? The **square** green one by the fishmonger's? The **cylindrical** bronze one by the ironmonger's? The tall red **bottle-shaped** one by the cakemonger's? Each was so tempting—but how to choose?

Then, suddenly, they saw it. Their eyes widened with delight and expectation, for each knew that if they could knock over only one bin, it would have to be this one. It stood, as high as a house and twice as wide, at the very end of the street, gleaming silver in the moonlight. As they stared, the delirious badgers could imagine it crashing to the ground in a more **crashy** and **binny** way than any bin they had ever knocked over.

They looked at one another and exchanged excited nods; and then they

In one tremendous mob they ran, hurling themselves towards this **bin of all bins**, their hearts filled with **ecstasy** and **rapture** at the naughtiness of what they were about to do. Faster and faster they raced, until they could not have stopped if they wanted to; and just before that moment of sheer joy when they collided with it and knocked it **tumbling** and **clattering** to the ground . . .

shouted Stinkbomb and Ketchup-Face together, and they and King Toothbrush Weasel, and the frightened chicken, and all the villagers pulled as hard as they could on the cleverly-disguised night-coloured rope which was tied to the enormous dustbin; and the little shopping trolley, in its cunning hiding place under the bin, heaved and squeaked with all its might; and the bin rolled right out of the way.

`Aaaaargh!'

yelled the shocked badgers as, unable to stop, they ran headlong into the village jail, which had been hidden behind the bin all the time. `Oh, no!' they added, as Malcolm the Cat leapt up and slammed the door behind them.

'Caught you, you horrid old badgers!' Ketchup-Face said happily. 'And now you have to be in jail for ever and ever!'

'Well, not for ever and ever,' said Stinkbomb. 'Just until the end of your sentence.'

'That doesn't seem very long,' said Ketchup-Face. 'Just till the end of a sentence? It should be till the end of the whole story, at least. Except that's not very long now.'

'Actually,' said King Toothbrush Weasel, 'the penalty for treacle is to stay in jail until halfway through the story after next.'

'That seems fair,' said the little shopping trolley.

'Buk-*AWWWWK!*' said the frightened chicken.

'Wait a minute,' said Malcolm the Cat. 'These don't look like the same badgers to me. Maybe we should let them go.' He opened the jail door again. Then he said, 'Or maybe they are the same badgers,' and shut it. 'On the other hand . . . '

'Grrr!' growled Rolf the Badger. 'You just wait!'

'Yeah!' agreed Harry the Badger. 'We'll get out of here, and then we'll knock over all the dustbins in town, and do some other **evil** things we haven't thought of yet!'

chorused all the other badgers, except Stewart the Badger who had found the jail's games cupboard.

'Hey!' he said. 'Anyone want a game of Monopoly?'

'Bagsy be the little car!' said all the other badgers at once.

'Come on, everyone!' said King Toothbrush Weasel. 'Time to celebrate! Let's go to the Loose Chippings Cafe!'

'Hooray!'

said Stinkbomb and Ketchup-Face,

and the little shopping trolley, and all the villagers.

'Buk-*AWWWWK!*' said the frightened chicken.

'Grrrrr!'

said the badgers; and they began to drive the little car too fast round the Monopoly board, knocking over the houses and hotels as they went.

So it was that, a few minutes later, Stinkbomb and Ketchup-Face found themselves in the Loose Chippings Cafe, surrounded by admiring villagers and being bought all manner of **lovely treats** as they told everyone the story of their adventures and King Toothbrush Weasel pinned medals on them. In the cafe all was **warm** and **cosy** and **friendly**; and in the distance they could hear the happy sound of the jail door opening and closing repeatedly. Only one more thing, they thought, was needed to make the scene completely perfect.

And then, to their delight, they saw two famil-
iar shapes silhouetted on the frosted glass of the
cafe door; and the door began to open.

'Mum! Dad!' cried Stinkbomb.

'HELLO, MY DARLINGS!'

came their mother's
voice from outside.

'CAN WE COME IN?
HAS THE STORY
FINISHED YET?'

'Yes,' said
Ketchup-Face happily.

'Would
to hear
Son

you like my new g?

Blueberry Jam

by Ketchup-Face

Allegro

Blue - ber - ry jam

f

Blue - ber - ry jam

Blue-ber-ry jam   Blue-ber-ry jam

Blue-ber-ry   blue-ber-ry   blue-ber-ry jam

180

Blue - y blue - y blue - y blue - y

Blue - y blue - y blue-ber - ry jam

Blue-ber - ry jam Blue-ber - ry

jam Blue-ber - ry JAM!
ff *fff*

181

Acknowledgements

With thanks to everyone who's ever done, said, or been anything that has ended up being pinched by me and put into this book. Particular thanks go to:
Toby Perot for inspiring Ketchup-Face's song; Saskia Honey Jarlett McAndrews for her exceptional King-naming skills; my old & dear friend John Sandford, wondering if you'll remember which bit I pinched from you; and Malcolm the cat for being a cat called Malcolm.

And particular particular thanks go to Noah & Cara for all the inspiration & ideas, help & encouragement, and for lighting up my life even when the curtains are drawn & I'm trying to sleep. Without you, there'd be no Great Kerfuffle. J.D.

Photo © Michael Dannenberg

John Dougherty

(Author)

I like to write about Stinkbomb and Ketchup-Face!

Illustration by Stanley Tazzyman

David Tazzyman

(Illustrator)

I like to draw badgers!

Ready for more great stories?
Try one of these . . .

Ooh look . . . more funny books, but none of these have badgers in them!